Lion C___
Share

written by Dr. Mary Manz Simon
illustrated by Phyllis Harris

© 2004 Mary Manz Simon. © 2004 Standard Publishing, Cincinnati, Ohio. A division of Standex International Corporation. All rights reserved. Sprout logo is a trademark of Standard Publishing. First Virtues™ is a trademark of Standard Publishing. Printed in China. Project editor: Amy Beveridge. Design: Robert Glover and Suzanne Jacobson. Scripture taken from the HOLY BIBLE, NEW INTERNATIONAL VERSION®. NIV® Copyright © 1973,1978,1984 by the the International Bible Society. Used by permission of Zondervan. All rights reserved. ISBN 0-7847-1576-9

10 09 08 07 06 05 04   9 8 7 6 5 4 3 2

Standard Publishing
cincinnati, ohio

www.standardpub.com

Lion, Lion, share today, what the Bible has to say...

God's Word says
that we should share
from our hearts,
to show we care.

If I have some
coins to spend,
I can share them
with my friend.

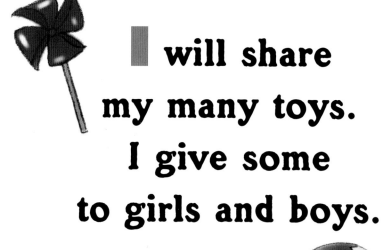

I will share
my many toys.
I give some
to girls and boys.

When I get
a brand new book,
I will say,
"Here, take a look."

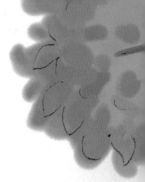

If I see
you're hungry, too,
I will share
my snack with you.

And if someone
looks so sad,
I share smiles
to make him glad.

For I care
from inside out.
That's what
sharing's all about.

God gives me
so much to share.
How do you show
that you care?

"Be generous and willing to share."
1 Timothy 6:18